I0765544

BRAVE STEPS

A FAMILY'S LOVE AND STRENGTH

BY
IISHA COLLIER

It was a bright and sunny day in May.
The sky stretched wide and blue, and the warm sun kissed my cheeks as I woke up. It felt like the clouds had parted just to let the sunshine through. Today was a special day-Mom had planned something wonderful! We were going to visit Grandma, attend a cookout, and spend time outside enjoying the beautiful weather.

I ran outside to play. The grass felt soft under my feet, and the smell of blooming flowers filled the air. Meanwhile, my mom laid down to rest her allergies made her sneeze a lot.

Mom had only been resting for a little while, when her phone rang. I saw her face change as she listened. Her eyes filled with worry. She sat up quickly, pressing the phone to her ear. When she finished the call, she took a deep breath and looked at my brother Corwyn and I.

Even though she said he was safe, my heartfelt heavy. Mom told us she had to fly to Walter Reed Hospital to be with Dad in Washington, D.C. She hugged us tightly and promised to call every day. Grandma took care of us while Mom was gone, making sure we went to pre-school and stayed on our routine. Each night, Grandma helped us say prayers for Dad.

Mom kept her promise-she called everyday. She let us talk to Dad, and he told us he missed us. His voice sounded a little tired, but he still made jokes, which made me smile. After a few days, Mom told us that we were going to visit Dad in Washington, D.C. Auntie Sasha, Mom's friend, would drive us there.

We packed our bags, filling them with clothes, toys, and our favorite stuffed animals.

The car ride was long, and we were excited, but something unexpected happened. In Pennsylvania, the car suddenly started to wobble-Auntie Sasha pulled over. "We've got a flat tire," she said with a sigh. We waited by the side of the road while the tow repair man came to help us. I watched the cars zoom past, each one a blur of colors. Finally, the tire was fixed, and we were back on the road!

When we arrived at Walter Reed Hospital,
I felt nervous. I wasn't sure what to expect.
Mom explained that Dad had to stay covered up
because of his injuries.
WALTER REED ARMY
MEDICAL CENTER

Machines were connected to his hands and legs, beeping softly in the room. Corwyn, always full of energy, tried swinging from Dad's hospital bed. Before we knew it-BEEP! BEEP! BEEP! one of the machines came unplugged. A nurse rushed in to fix it while Mom gave Corwyn a look that said, "Be careful!

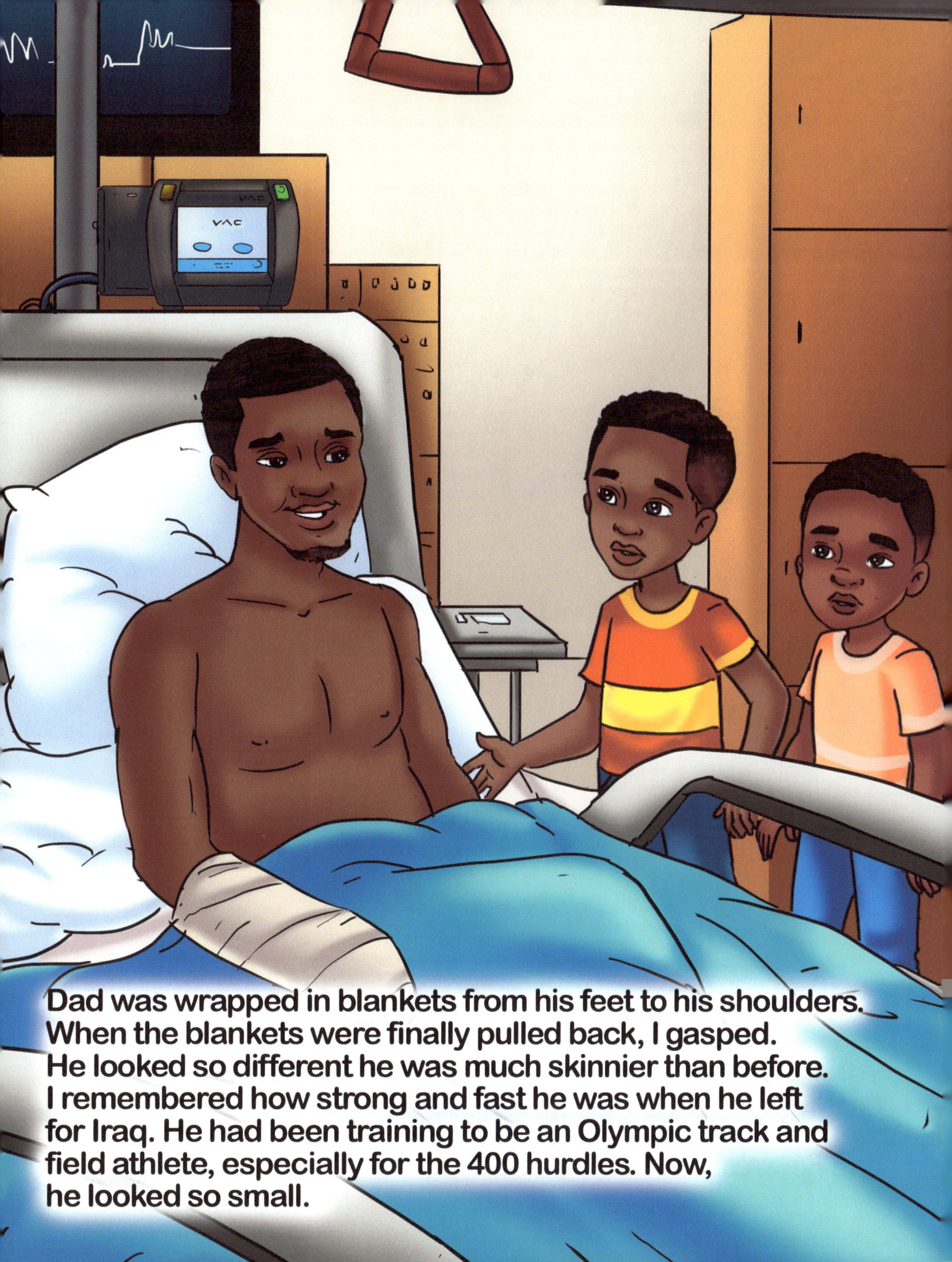

Dad was wrapped in blankets from his feet to his shoulders.
When the blankets were finally pulled back, I gasped.
He looked so different he was much skinnier than before.
I remembered how strong and fast he was when he left
for Iraq. He had been training to be an Olympic track and
field athlete, especially for the 400 hurdles. Now,
he looked so small.

Auntie Sasha stayed for the weekend, but then she had to go back home for work. She took Corwyn, my little brother, back to Ohio with her. I stayed with Mom and Dad at the hospital.

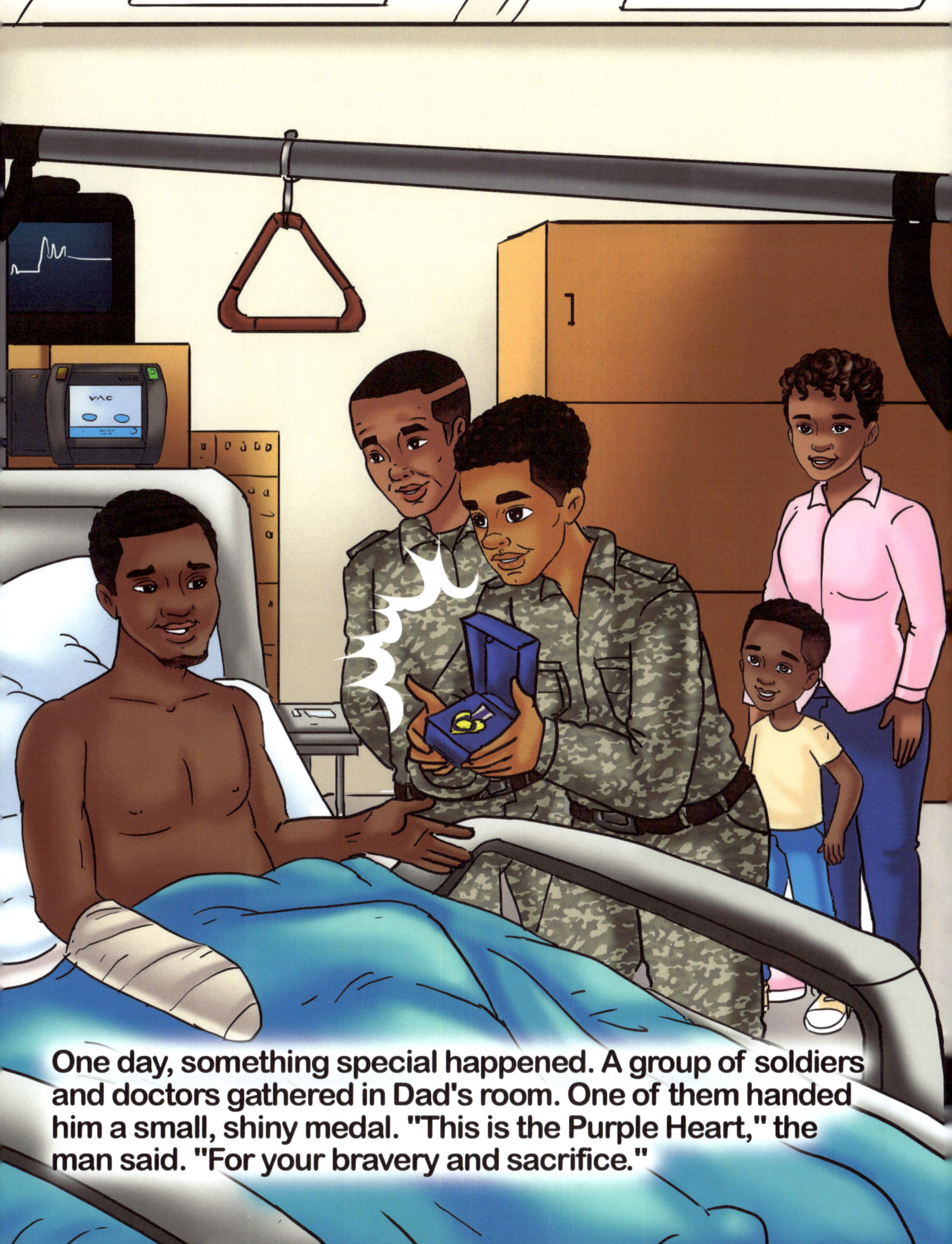

One day, something special happened. A group of soldiers and doctors gathered in Dad's room. One of them handed him a small, shiny medal. "This is the Purple Heart," the man said. "For your bravery and sacrifice."

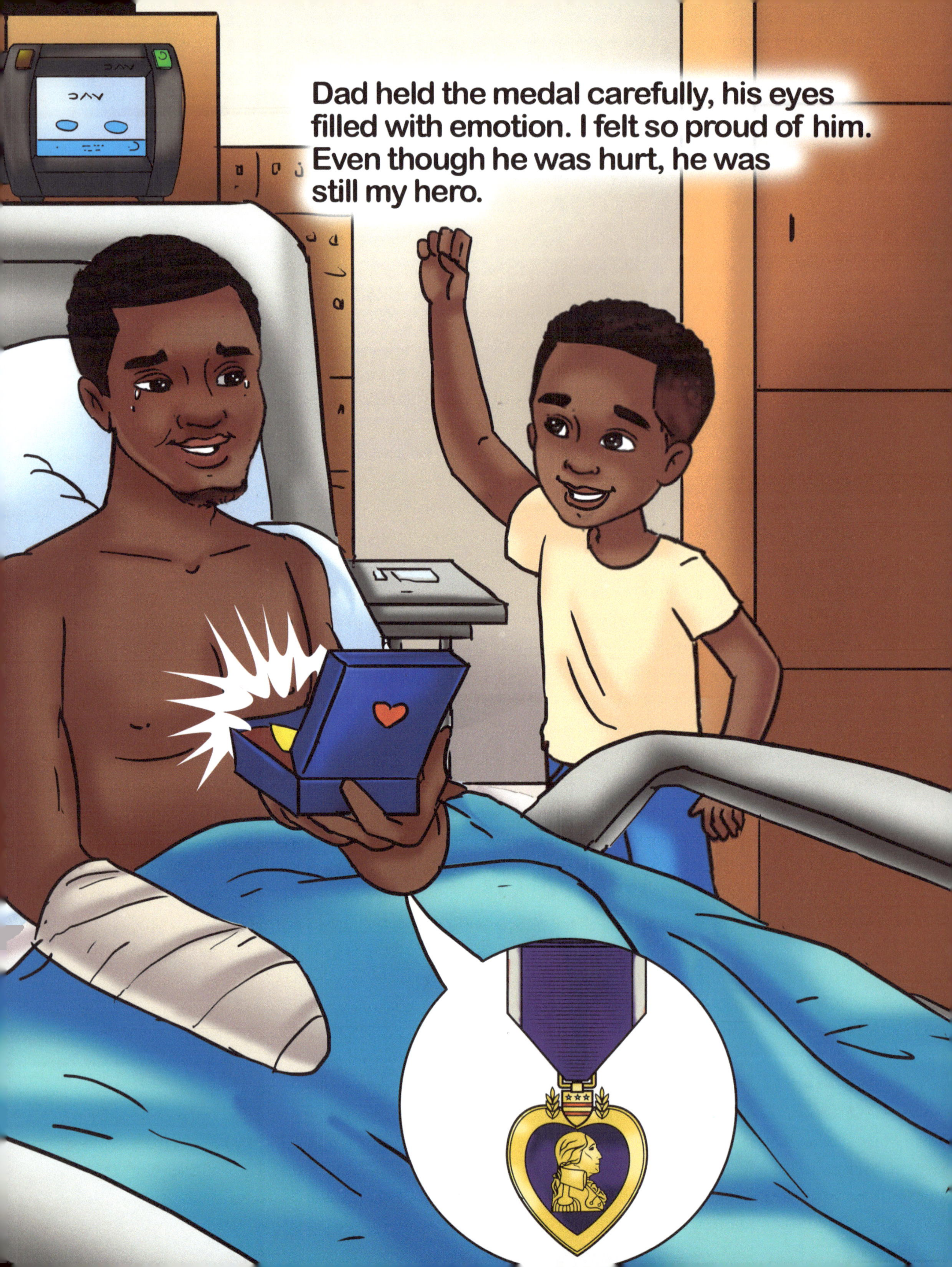
Dad held the medal carefully, his eyes filled with emotion. I felt so proud of him. Even though he was hurt, he was still my hero.

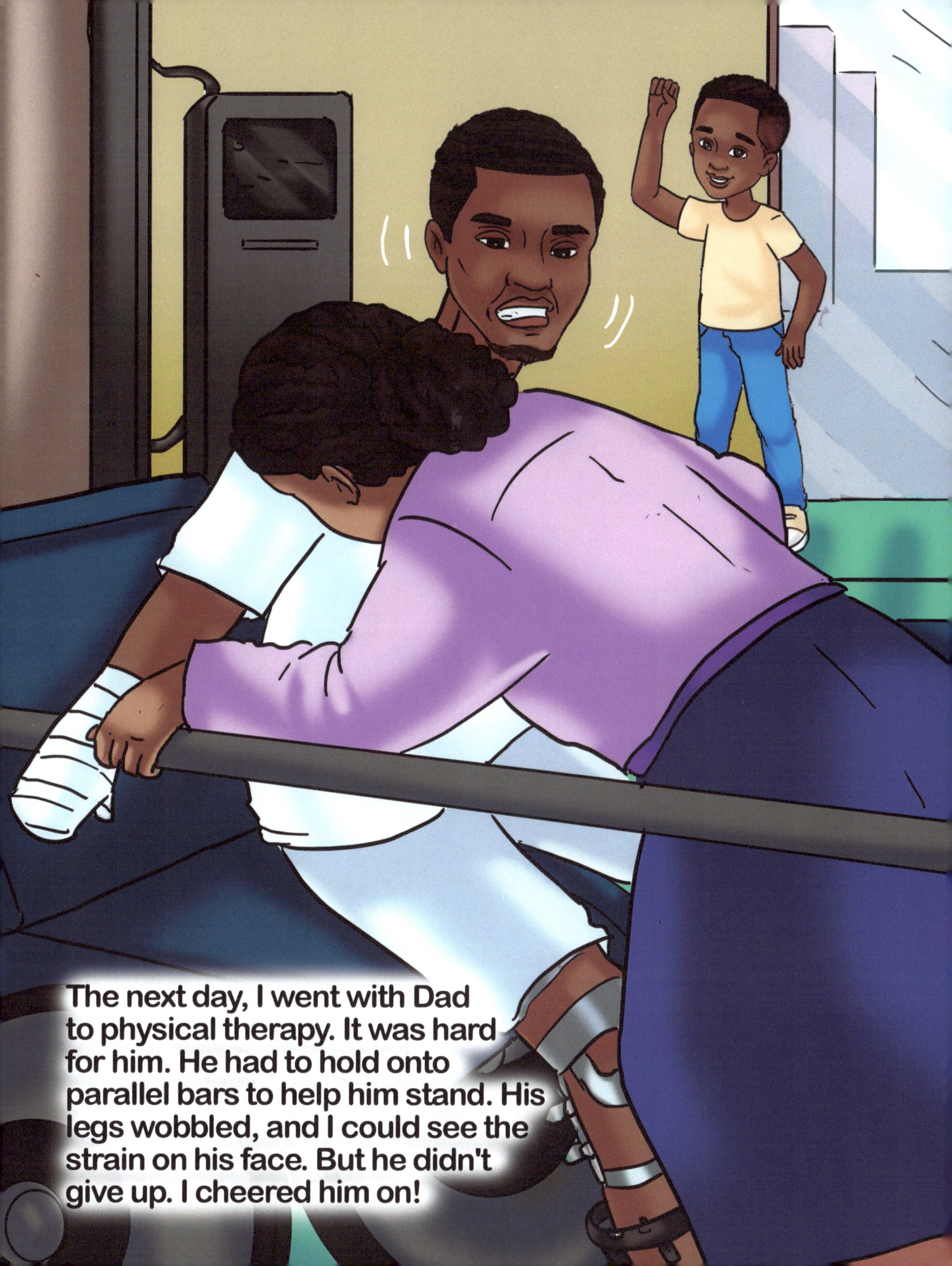
The next day, I went with Dad to physical therapy. It was hard for him. He had to hold onto parallel bars to help him stand. His legs wobbled, and I could see the strain on his face. But he didn't give up. I cheered him on!

HERO!

That day, I realized something important. Heroes aren't just strong because they fight battles-they're strong because they never stop trying. And my dad? He was the strongest person I knew.

On the way back to his room that day, Dad cried.
Mom leaned over and said, "You have to be strong and be
the man we are used to you being. Everything is not going
to come easy or overnight. You have to work hard for
everything if you want to walk again. We believe in you,
and you can do this."

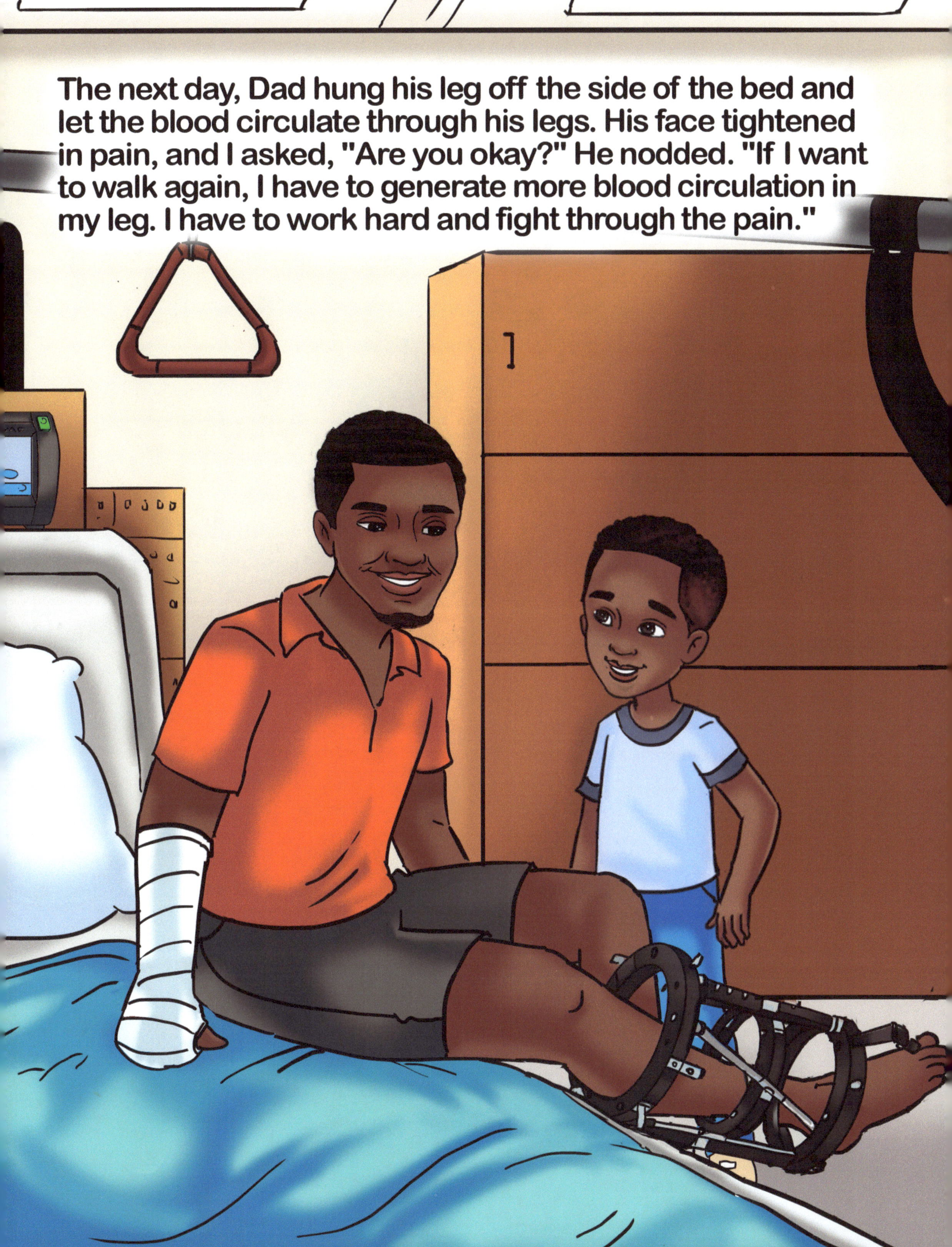

The next day, Dad hung his leg off the side of the bed and let the blood circulate through his legs. His face tightened in pain, and I asked, "Are you okay?" He nodded. "If I want to walk again, I have to generate more blood circulation in my leg. I have to work hard and fight through the pain."

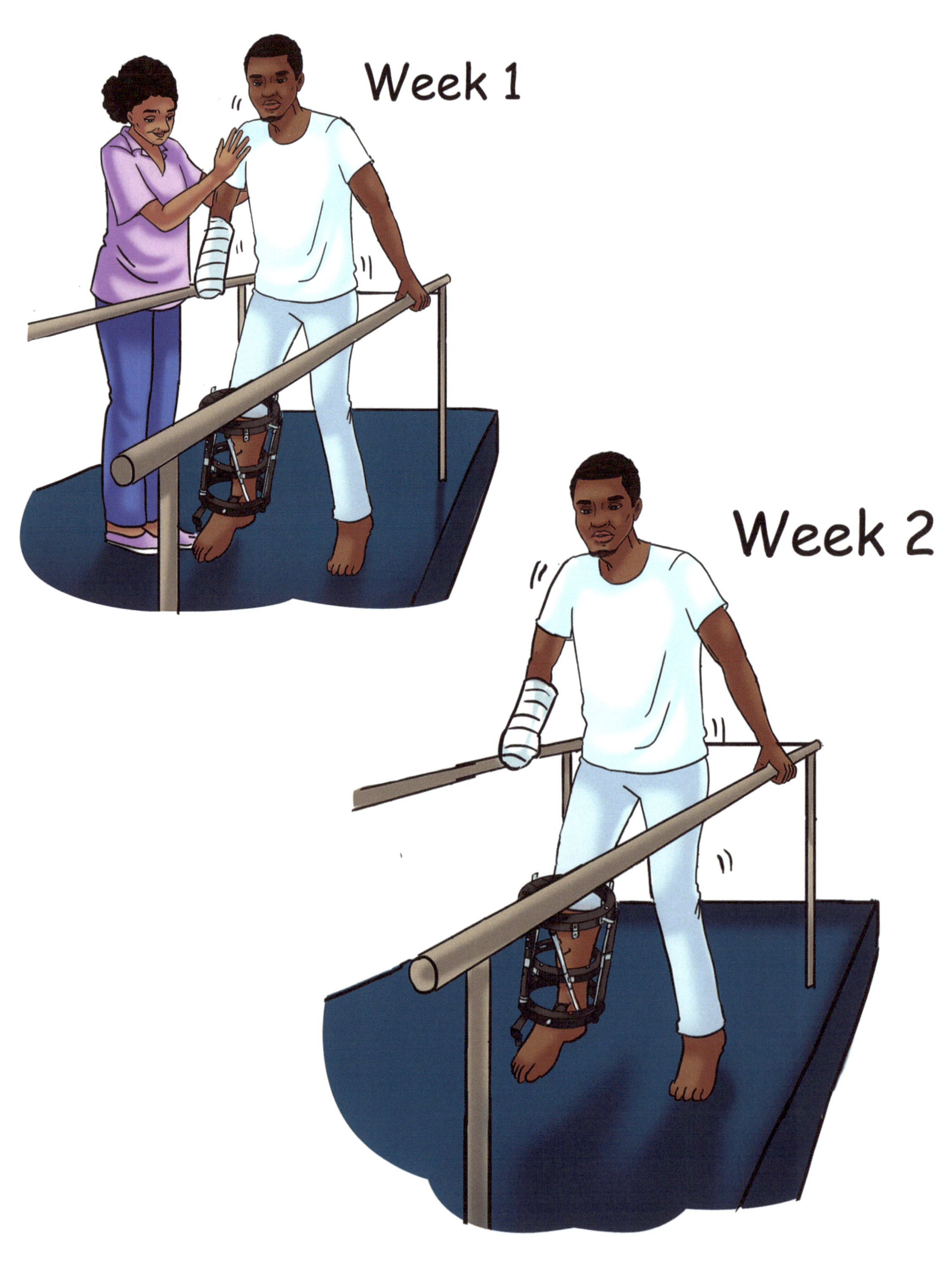

Week 1
Week 2

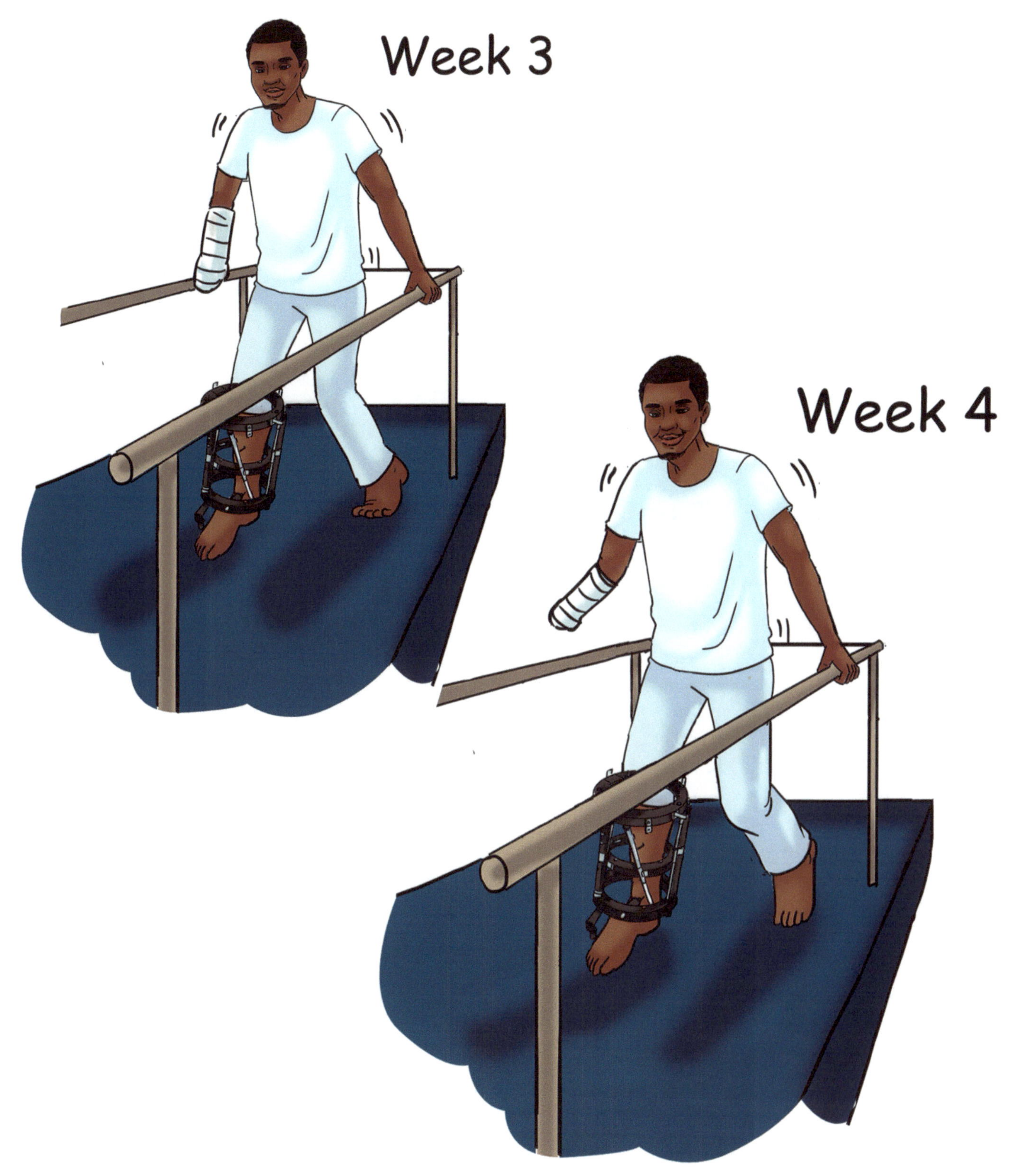

Over the next several weeks, I watched Dad practice this drill of hanging his leg off the side of the bed every day and go to physical therapy. Each day, he pushed himself little more. Eventually, each day he was able to take a couple more steps.

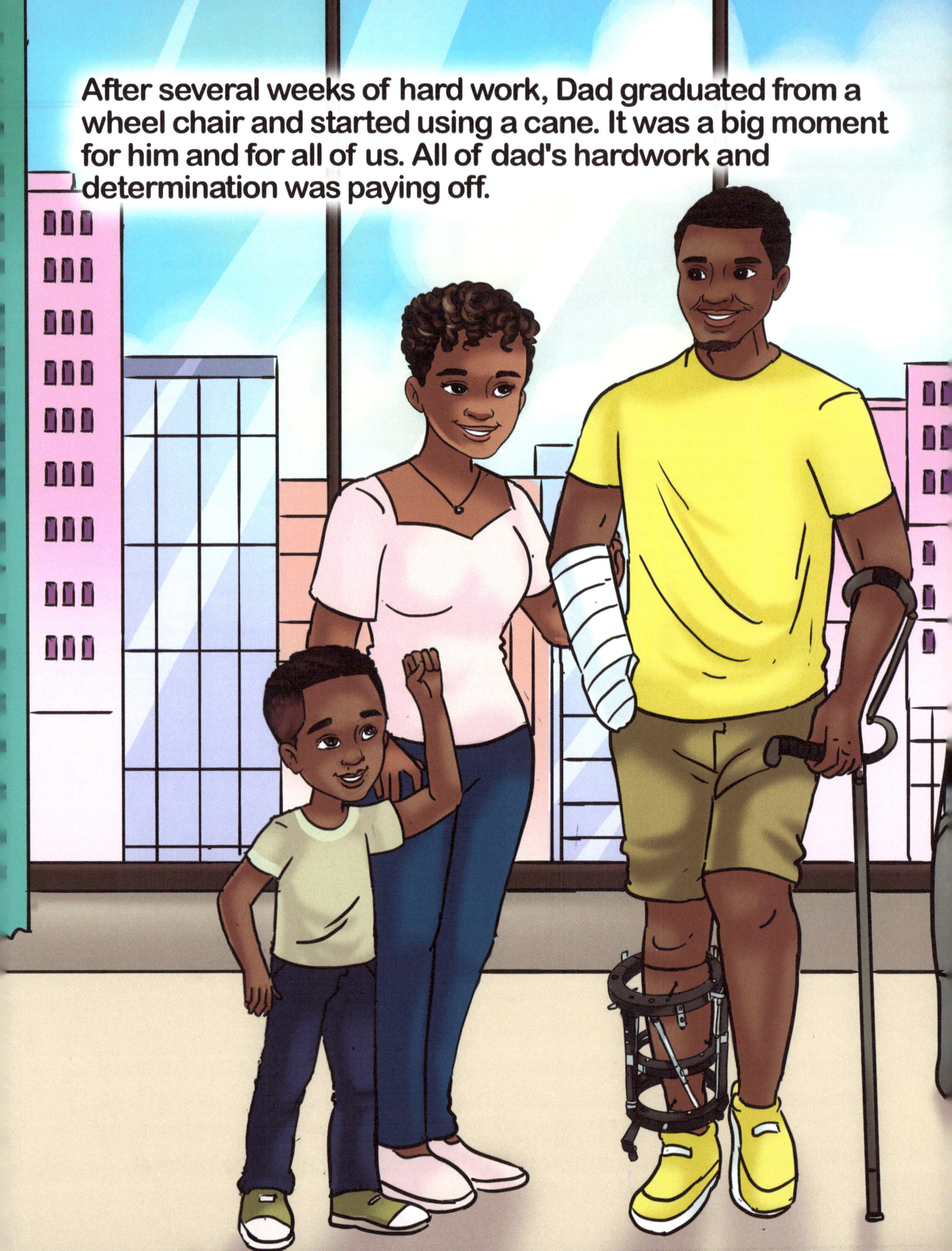

After several weeks of hard work, Dad graduated from a wheel chair and started using a cane. It was a big moment for him and for all of us. All of dad's hardwork and determination was paying off.

By the time my little brother Corwyn came back to the hospital, Dad was walking around outside with a cane. He smiled proudly as he took steps outside in the fresh air. It was a long journey, but he never gave up. To me, he would always be the strongest man in the world!

Because every military family deserves connection, strength, and hope.

About the Author: Iisha Collier is a dynamic author, educator, and military family advocate whose work bridges personal experience with professional expertise to deliver powerful, actionable insights for families navigating the challenges of military life. With 18 years of educational experience spanning roles as a preschool teacher, regular education classroom teacher, literacy intervention specialist, instructional specialist, assistant principal, curriculum director, and adjunct professor, Iisha offers a deep and well-rounded perspective on learning and leadership.

She holds a bachelor's degree in Early Childhood Education, dual master's degrees in Elementary Education (Literacy Focus) and Educational Administration (Urban Education Focus), and specialized credentials in reading, gifted education, diversity and inclusion, and educational leadership (principal and superintendent licensure).

Iisha's writing combines heartfelt storytelling, to help military families build resilience, maintain connection, and thrive through deployment and reintegration. Her mission is to equip parents, educators, and communities with the knowledge and support they need — making her an essential voice for anyone invested in strengthening military family well-being.

This book is dedicated to the brave men and women who serve, and to the families who stand beside them— your love, courage, and strength light the way through every storm.

To my family, friends and amazing husband-Sgt. Corwyn Collier Sr. and children Malachi Collier and Corwyn Jr., whose unwavering support and resilience inspired every page of this story. You are my heart, my hope, and my Strength. Thank you for showing the world what it truly means to be brave.

Publishing: Collier Elite Publishing, 2025